friends

Other Friends ⓐ bang on the door™© titles

friends united

Coming Soon

friends again

First published in 2003 in Great Britain
by HarperCollins*Publishers* Ltd.

1 3 5 7 9 8 6 4 2

ISBN: 0 00 715212 4

www.bangonthedoor.com

Text © 2003 HarperCollins*Publishers* Ltd/Narinder Dhami

The HarperCollins website address is: www.harpercollins.co.uk

Printed and bound in Great Britain by Clays Ltd, St Ives plc.

bang on the door™ ©

friends

Collins

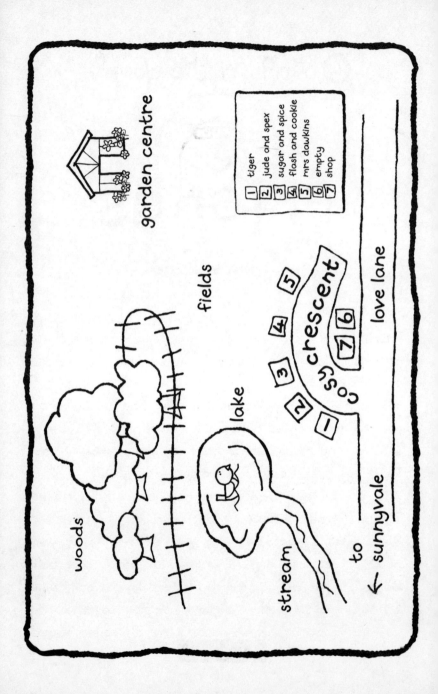

Chapter One

"Flash! Quick, over here!" Jude was jumping up and down in the middle of the street like a mad thing, waving his arms. "Pass it back!"

"Sorry?" Flash looked up dreamily. The football shot past him and bobbed across the tarmac towards Tiger.

"Ta very much," she said. Then she winked at me. "Come on, Spex. Let's see if we can get a goal!"

I pushed my glasses up my nose, and set off after Tiger. I'm not as brilliant at football as my brother Jude. Well, I guess he *is* a year older than me and about a metre taller! OK, maybe not *quite* that tall. But ever since he got offered a trial with the local boys' team, Sunnyvale Juniors, he thinks he plays for England!

Tiger slotted the ball across to me. I was just about

to head towards the two wheelie bins, which were the goalposts, when Jude came up behind me. He barged me off the ball, and ran away with it.

"Foul!" called Cookie, Flash's sister. She was sitting on the pink-painted wall of Number One, holding her brother's camera.

Jude stopped, put his hands on his hips and glared at her. I tried not to laugh as Cookie smiled sweetly back at him.

"Who made *you* the referee?" he demanded.

"Nobody," replied Cookie. "I was *just being helpful.*"

"What do you know about football, anyway?" demanded Jude.

"Ooh, lots!" There was a wicked glint in Cookie's eyes as she grinned at Jude.

"OK, so how many players are there on a team?" Jude asked.

"Eleven," replied Cookie promptly.

"What's the name of Manchester United's ground?"

"Old Trafford."

Flash, Tiger and I were trying not to laugh. Jude was starting to look a bit narked by now, while Cookie was still smiling sweetly.

"Go on, ask me anything you like," she said.

But Jude already had the look on his face of someone who knew he'd lost the argument about – oh – five minutes ago! "Forget it," he muttered.

"Are we playing football or not?" Tiger asked impatiently, flicking her straight, strawberry-blonde hair out of her eyes.

"We're playing football," Jude agreed quickly. "Sorry."

We all moved back into the middle of the street. Nope, don't worry, we're not playing in the traffic! Cosy Crescent in Sunnyvale, where we all live, is a cul-de-sac. There's only six houses in a kind of semicircle, and then the shop at Number Seven. So it's a great place to play all kinds of games. We were playing outside a lot at the moment because it was the Easter holidays and the weather was brilliant. Our Oldies (parents to you) don't get all wound up either because they know we're safe.

"Right, watch this," Jude called, scooping the ball up with his foot. He juggled it from knee to knee, doing keepy-uppies, and then shot a sideways glance at Tiger to make sure she was watching him. Jude *loves* to impress.

"Let me get a photo of that," Flash said eagerly, as Jude flicked the ball into the air and began keeping it up with his head. "It'll be a good action shot." Flash is mad about taking photos, even though he's only got a dead old camera that his dad gave him. They usually come out pretty well though. Flash and Cookie's dad is a photographer, and Flash wants to be one too, when he grows up.

"Look at him!" Tiger whispered, laughing, in my ear. Jude was trying to grin widely at the camera while keeping the ball in the air. Then he let it drop down and started juggling it from knee to knee again, while Flash clicked away.

"He's good though, isn't he?" I whispered back. OK, so Jude was a bit of a show-off, but he was still my brother and I was proud of him.

Tiger stood there, watching, with her hands on her hips. Then suddenly she darted forward and nicked the ball off Jude's knee. Jude's mouth dropped open as she sped off with it. He wasn't expecting that – and neither was I!

Jude set off after Tiger, but it was too late. She banged the ball between the two wheelie bins and scored. The ball flew high in the air, sailed through the gap between Numbers Three and Four, over the fence and into the field behind the houses.

"I'll get it," Cookie called. She jumped down off the wall and ran over to the fence. It's only low, so it's pretty easy to climb over. There's a gate a few hundred yards away, but none of us can ever be bothered to use it.

"Be careful," Flash called, as Cookie scrambled over the fence. He kind of likes to play the older brother a lot of the time, but I'm not so sure Cookie needs looking after. Flash thinks she does, because she's only six. But it's more like *she* looks after Flash (although he doesn't realise it).

Cookie nodded and waved at him. Then she did three perfect cartwheels across the grass, one after the other, towards the football. Ever since she started doing gymnastics at school, she can't stay the right way up for five minutes!

"Two-all now, isn't it?" Tiger asked breezily.

"That wasn't fair," Jude grumbled. "I wasn't ready."

I went over to the fence and watched Cookie chasing after the ball, which was still bobbing across the grass. I forgot to tell you that Cosy Crescent is right on the edge of Sunnyvale, and behind the houses is the countryside. There are big fields stretching away in every direction, and there's a wood, a stream and a small lake where people come and fish. The fields are private property, but the lady who owns them, old Mrs Dawkins, doesn't mind people using them. She lives in Cosy Crescent too, at Number Five with all her cats (about ten at the last count). She's OK, but she tends to keep herself to herself.

"Here, Spex." Cookie handed me the football, and I gave her a hand to pull her back over the fence. Then I booted the ball over to my brother.

"We need some more players," Jude muttered, trying very hard not to look annoyed that Tiger had scored. "It's useless with just four people. We need some goalies."

"Well, has anyone made friends with those twins

yet?" Tiger swivelled round on her heel and pointed across the road at Number Three.

"What twins?" Flash asked absently. He was busy fiddling with his camera.

"The ones who moved in four weeks ago!" Jude grinned

"Oh, *those* twins." Flash began to polish his camera lens with his sleeve.

We all stared at Number Three. Although none of the houses in Cosy Crescent is posh, Number Three was the most run-down of the lot. It had been empty for a long time, but about a month ago a new family had moved in. All we knew about them was that they were called the Harts, and there was a dad and twin girls. The twins looked gobsmackingly identical. You really *couldn't* tell them apart.

"They're in our year at school, aren't they, Flash?" I said. "Only they're not in our class, so I don't know them yet."

"I've seen their dad a couple of times, going in and out of the house." Jude pulled a face. "He looks a bit funny. Long hair and this really old coat."

"That's not their dad," I cut in. "That's their lodger. I heard Mum and Gran talking about it. His name's Tom something."

"Yeah." Cookie backed me up. "Their dad's that man with no hair and a really smiley face."

Right at that moment the twins unexpectedly came round the side of the house from their back garden. It was kind of embarrassing because there we all were, standing in a row staring at them. We looked away and shuffled our feet, but the twins didn't look embarrassed at all. They both flicked back their long blonde pigtails at exactly the same moment, and carried on chatting to each other.

"Let's go and say hello," Tiger suggested.

"Ooh, yes," Cookie agreed.

Girls are always better at doing that sort of stuff, aren't they? Don't know why! Jude and I hung back trying to look cool, as Tiger and Cookie marched off. I don't think Flash was even listening. He was too busy with his camera!

"Hi." Tiger smiled at the two girls. "Welcome to Cosy Crescent. I'm Tiger from Number One."

"And I'm Cookie, Number Four," Cookie added. She turned and pointed at us. "And those two boys trying to look cool over there are Jude and Spex. Oh, and the other one's my brother Flash."

"Hello," said one of the twins.

"Nice to meet you," said the other.

"We haven't really got to know anyone round here yet," the first one continued. "Because..."

"...we haven't lived here that long," the second one finished.

Our mouths fell open. We must have looked like a row of goldfish! It was very strange seeing two people who looked the same, sounded the same and finished off each other's sentences. It was as if one of them was a perfect clone of the other.

"What are your names?" Tiger asked, looking dazed.

"I'm Sugar," said the first one.

The other twin stared at her. "No, *I'm* Sugar, aren't I?"

"No, you're Spice," the first one replied.

"No, *you're* Spice," the other one retorted.

"Am I?" The first girl looked puzzled.

"Oh, very funny," Jude snorted, but he was laughing. Both girls cocked their heads to one side at exactly the same moment, and stared at us wickedly.

"We can't even tell *ourselves* apart!" the first one laughed.

"Is that why you wear those different-coloured patches on your jeans?" Cookie chimed in.

Trust Cookie to notice! One of the girls had a yellow patch on the knee of her frayed jeans, and the other had a green one.

The twins looked at each other, their eyes twinkling.

"She's got us!" the first one grinned, tapping her yellow patch. "OK, I'm Sugar."

"And I'm Spice," the twin with the green patch added. "We have to wear these..."

12

"...because our dad can't tell us apart either," Sugar laughed.

"What about if you want to confuse him?" I asked. "Do you switch clothes?"

Spice winked at me. "Sometimes," she replied. "Just to make life more interesting!"

"Do you want to play football with us?" Jude asked. "We could do with some extra players."

"OK," Spice agreed. "As long as..."

"...we don't have to go in goal," Sugar finished off, and Spice nodded.

Jude blinked. All this double talk could get a bit mind-blowing! "OK," he said. "Tiger and Flash can go in goal. Sugar, you play with Tiger, and Spice, you can play with me."

Laughing and joking, we all headed back into the road. Jude was just about to knock the ball into play when the front door of Number Three flew open and the twins' dad dashed out. Cookie had described him as having a smiley face, but he didn't look very smiley at the moment. He looked pretty worried.

"Sugar! Spice!" he yelled, rushing down the front garden to the gate. "Have you seen Tom?"

Both girls shook their heads.

"He said he was going shopping," Sugar replied.

"What's the matter, Dad?" Spice wanted to know.

Mr Hart looked very upset. "The lodger's done a

13

bunk, that's what! He's upped and cleared off, without paying me any rent. All he's left behind are a scrawled note, a few old clothes and an old, broken-down computer!"

Chapter Two

"Oh, *Dad!*" Sugar and Spice said together. They ran over to him, looking upset.

Jude picked the ball up and tucked it under his arm. "I told you that lodger guy looked a bit strange," he said to me under his breath.

"Are you sure, Dad?" Sugar asked.

"Maybe he *has* just gone shopping," Spice added.

"Well, if he has, he's taken his suitcase and most of his clothes with him!" Mr Hart replied glumly. "Anyway, the note indicates he's not coming back, it's very apologetic, but not much help to us. I didn't ask him for any rent in advance, either. He was supposed to pay me at the end of the month."

Sugar groaned. "Why didn't you get a deposit, Dad?"

"Because he said he didn't have any money until he started his new job," Mr Hart muttered sheepishly.

"Dad, you didn't lend him any money, did you?" Spice asked sternly.

Mr Hart looked guilty. "Well, he *said* he'd pay me back as soon as he started work..."

Jude raised his eyebrows at the rest of us who were standing silently by, listening. "That was a pretty silly thing to do," he whispered.

"The twins' dad was just trying to be kind and help someone out," Tiger whispered back crossly. "There's nothing wrong with that, is there?"

"Er... no, course not," Jude backtracked quickly.

The twins put their arms round their dad and gave him a hug. "Don't worry, Dad," said Spice comfortingly. "We'll manage."

"Maybe you could sell the stuff that your lodger left behind," Jude said, trying to be helpful. Then he beamed as Tiger flashed him a quick smile.

But Mr Hart was looking doubtful. "The clothes aren't up to much," he said. "And I don't know anything about computers. This one doesn't even work."

"Spex knows all about computers," Tiger broke in, patting me on the shoulder. "He's in the computer club at school. He's so good, that sometimes even the teachers ask him to fix them if they go wrong!"

I went all hot and fiddled with my glasses as

everyone turned to look at me. "I'm not *that* good," I muttered. We didn't have a computer at home because Mum couldn't afford to get us one, and I'd only ever used one at school.

But Mr Hart was staring at me hopefully. "Well, maybe you could just have a look at it and tell me if you think it's worth anything, son," he said. "I'd be very grateful."

"Come on, Spex!" Suddenly I had a twin on either side of me. Grabbing my hands, Sugar and Spice pulled me down the path and through the front door before I even knew what was happening. Mr Hart and the others followed.

Number Three was almost exactly the same as our house, Number Two, but it was a lot shabbier. And our house isn't exactly a palace. The wallpaper in the hall was peeling off in places, and the old carpets had been ripped up, leaving bare floorboards. There were pots of paint and brushes and packets of wallpaper paste lying around.

"We've got a lot of work to do around the place," Mr Hart said as the twins hurried me upstairs.

The lodger's room was the smallest one. It had already been decorated in pale blue, and it smelled of fresh paint. There was a bed and a wardrobe with the doors hanging open, as if someone had packed and gone off in a big hurry. The coat hangers were all empty except for a long, dirty, black coat and a crumpled blue shirt, and there was a pair of battered old shoes on the floor.

"I'm not surprised he left that old coat behind," I heard Jude whisper to the others. "It looks like something the cat dragged in!"

"And I bet it smells like it too," Cookie added.

The computer was sitting on a small desk under the window, alongside a scanner and a printer. But I could tell that they were really old. And I mean *old*. If this computer were a human, it would be collecting its old age pension!

I turned to Mr Hart. "Have you tried switching it on?" I asked. You'd be surprised how often people forget to do that!

Mr Hart nodded. "I can't get it to work at all," he said despairingly.

I bent down to take a look under the table. There were several *big* boxes stacked under there, all filled with sheets of white paper. "Er... it isn't actually switched on at the wall," I said politely, pointing to the socket.

"Dad!" Sugar and Spice began to giggle. "You're hopeless!"

I flicked the electricity on, and the computer fired up immediately.

"It works!" Mr Hart gasped, looking pleased.

We all stood there as the computer clunked away, getting started up.

"Why is it taking so *long* ?" Cookie moaned after a few minutes.

"Because it's old," I replied. "But it looks like it works OK."

I checked the scanner and the printer. They were both hooked up properly, and as far as I could tell, they worked too.

"So how much do you think I'd get for it?" Mr Hart asked eagerly.

Now I had to give him the bad news.

"Not much," I said as kindly as I could, but his face dropped. "It's just too old and too slow. You could keep it for yourself, though."

Mr Hart shook his head. "I'm not into computers, but maybe the girls would find it useful." Mr Hart looked quizzically at the twins, but they just grimaced. "We have enough computers at school, Dad," said Spice, and Sugar nodded in agreement.

"Oh, well, maybe I can find someone who wants to buy it, even if I only get twenty quid for it." But he didn't look at all hopeful.

We wandered down the stairs and back outside, leaving Mr Hart to put the lodger's clothes into a rubbish sack.

"Poor old Dad," Sugar sighed. "Things like this are always happening to him. The trouble is..."

"...he's just too NICE," Spice finished.

"Hey, look, guys," Flash said suddenly, "Great car!"

We all stared across the road at the car that was parked outside Number Five, old Mrs Dawkins' place. It looked really expensive. It was long and sleek and shiny and silver, with big chrome headlights and a sweeping, curved bonnet.

We all dashed over to take a look. Well, Jude, Flash and I did. The girls followed a bit more slowly, looking pretty uninterested.

"Wow! Look at that!" Jude breathed, peering in the side window. "Black leather seats, tinted electric windows, air-conditioning. And it's the turbo version!" Jude is really into cars.

"Yeah, twice as fast so you get twice as much pollution," Tiger sniffed, not looking at all impressed.

"Er... yeah, that's true," Jude agreed quickly. I grinned to myself. Tiger's pretty hot on environmental issues and stuff. She gets it from her parents who are kind of New Age hippies.

Flash lifted his camera. "Do you think the owner will let me take a picture?" he asked hopefully.

"Whose car is it anyway?" Cookie wanted to know.

We all turned as the front door of Number Five opened. As usual, a couple of cats made their escape before Mrs Dawkins appeared, and, as usual, she was wearing one of her hats. She's got about a million of them, and she wears them all the time. I've never, ever seen the top of her head! Today she wore a white beanie hat. And although it was warm, her tall, thin figure was draped about with waistcoats and shawls, and she also wore a thick skirt and Wellington boots. She was probably even thinner underneath all those layers of clothes.

"Who's that?" Spice asked, her eyes round.

"We haven't seen *her* before," Sugar added.

"That's Mrs Dawkins," Tiger explained. "She stays in her house a lot of the time with her cats."

"She looks a bit scary," Sugar whispered, staring at Mrs Dawkins' wrinkled face and piercing black eyes.

"No, she's all right," Tiger said. "Well, most of the time."

"She can be a bit strange," Jude remarked. "A bit... er... Spex, what does Mum call her?"

"A bit eccentric," I said helpfully.

"Sometimes she's really nice," Cookie chimed in. "And then other times she won't speak to us."

"That must be the guy who owns the car," Jude whispered, as a man followed the old lady outside.

It wasn't hard to guess. The man looked just as sleek and shiny and expensive as the car. He was wearing a blue suit, and carrying a flashy silver briefcase.

"Thanks for the tea," we heard him say as he walked down the path with Mrs Dawkins. "I'll be in touch." Then he spotted us standing by his car. I thought he might be a bit cross. We weren't doing anything, but, well, you know how snooty some people can be!

"Hello, kids." The man gave us a beaming smile. "Like the car?"

"It's excellent," Jude said eagerly, earning himself another dirty look from Tiger.

"You've got good taste, son," the man laughed.

"Do you mind if I take a picture of your car?" Flash asked.

The man shook his head. "Not at all. As long as I can be in it too."

"Oh, sure," Flash agreed.

We watched as Flash tinkered with his camera while the man stood next to the car, leaning his elbow on the roof. Flash took a couple of pictures, and then the man got in and drove off, waving at us in his rear-view mirror.

"He was nice," Cookie said to Mrs Dawkins. "What's his name?"

"Guy Lipman," The old lady replied in her throaty voice. She always sounded a bit hoarse. Tiger said it was because she didn't talk that much to anyone except her cats.

"What did he want?" Cookie asked curiously. Honestly, that kid can be a right nosy parker sometimes! But this time she'd gone too far. Old Mrs Dawkins drew herself up to her full height and glared at us all.

"None of your business," she snapped. Then she stomped back up the path, scooped up a cat under each arm and swept inside the house. The front door banged shut behind her.

"What's the matter with *her*?" Cookie sniffed.

"You were sticking your nose in where it's not wanted," Flash said, giving Cookie's ponytail a little pull. "You know she hates people asking questions."

Tiger was frowning. "I wonder who Mr Lipman is, though," she said, winding a strand of hair round her finger, the way she always does when she is thinking hard. "I mean, Mrs Dawkins never has any visitors, does she?"

"Look, let's get on with the game," Jude called impatiently, bouncing the ball up and down. That's my brother for you. He can't stand still for more than thirty seconds!

We moved back into the road between the wheelie bins. But suddenly a yell from the twins, who'd been whispering away to each other, made us nearly jump out of our skins.

"We've just had a brilliant idea!" Spice squealed.

"A *brilliant* idea!" Sugar agreed.

"That computer..." Spice began. "It seems..."

"...a shame to let it just sit there doing nothing," Sugar went on.

"So why don't we..."

"...use it to start up our own newspaper?"

Chapter Three

For a long moment there was a stunned silence. Then we all burst out talking at once.

"That's a totally cool idea," Tiger announced, her green eyes sparkling with excitement.

"We could include local news," I said eagerly, pushing my glasses up my nose.

"And sport," Jude added, booting the football between the wheelie bins. "Lots and lots of football."

"I could be the official photographer." Flash waved his camera.

"Can we have puzzles and jokes and lots of fun stuff?" Cookie wanted to know.

"We can make it really good," said Tiger. "But we'll have to do it *properly*."

"Tiger's right." Jude stroked his chin thoughtfully. "If we're going to do it, then it's got to be right. One of us will have to be the editor."

I tried not to look too keen. I was *dying* to be the editor of our newspaper. But I could tell from the look on Jude's face that he definitely thought that *he* was going to get the job. So I kept quiet.

"Hold on a minute though." Tiger turned to the twins who were beaming identically at us, looking very pleased that their idea had gone so well. "Sugar, Spice, do you think your dad will let us use the computer?"

The girls nodded at exactly the same moment. "Dad won't mind," Sugar began.

"He doesn't want to use it himself," Spice finished.

"Maybe we could give him something for it," Tiger suggested, shaking her fringe out of her eyes. "My mum and dad have an allotment, and they've always got fruit and veggies going spare. They give a lot of it away to the neighbours."

Jude nudged me. "Remember when the Cubbs had all those spare carrots?" he whispered in my ear. "We were eating them for weeks."

"I know," I said, "It's amazing we didn't all turn orange!"

"That would be great," Spice said eagerly.

"If your mum and dad don't mind," Sugar added.

"Let's go over to my place and I'll ask Mum," Tiger suggested.

Laughing and chatting loudly, we all ran over the road towards the Cubbs' house. It was the most eye-catching house in the whole crescent because it was a daffodil yellow colour. The windowsills were bright blue, and there was a large, colourful rainbow painted above the blue front door.

"Mum's down in the shed," Tiger told us, leading the way along the side of the house. She turned to the twins. "Mum's a potter," she explained. "That's where she works."

The bright-yellow shed was at the bottom of the Cubbs' long garden. Tiger opened the door, and there was Mrs Cubb sitting at her wheel, throwing a pot. She had clay all over her hands, and a big streak of it on her cheek.

"Hello!" Mrs Cubb smiled at us, brushing her long hair, which was exactly the same colour as Tiger's, out of her eyes. Then she spotted Sugar and Spice. "Oh, you're the twins from across the road, aren't you? Pleased to meet you."

"I'm Sugar," said Spice innocently.

"And I'm Spice," Sugar agreed.

Mrs Cubb blinked. "You're very alike, aren't you?" she said. "I'm sure I'll never be able to tell you apart!"

"I'm not really Sugar," Spice grinned.

"And I'm not really Spice," Sugar added.

"Stop it, you two!" Tiger laughed. "Mum, we wanted

to ask you something." And she explained about Tom, the lodger, leaving his computer behind, how the twins had come up with the idea of a local newspaper and whether we could pay Mr Hart with fruit and veggies from the Cubbs' allotment.

Mrs Cubb listened intently. "I think that's a wonderful idea," she said enthusiastically. "Of course you can have any spare produce we have. What's the newspaper going to be like?"

"We're going to have lots of local stuff," I told her.

"And football," Jude chimed in.

"Well, I hope you're going to include some serious Sunnyvale issues." Mrs Cubb rubbed her nose, leaving a smear of clay on it. "The pollution in the town is terrible with all those big lorries going through every day, for instance. You could start a campaign to stop that."

I glanced at Jude and saw him pull a face. I got the feeling he wanted the newspaper to be football, football and more football!

"What are we going to do now?" Cookie asked as we left the Cubbs' garden.

"Let's go and ask Dad about the computer," Sugar suggested.

"And then we can get started on the first issue of the paper," finished Spice.

My insides were churning with excitement as we hurried back across the road to the Harts' house. This was just about the most exciting thing that had ever happened in Cosy Crescent. Our own newspaper! So what if I didn't get to be editor? I was still really looking forward to getting started.

Mr Hart was glumly pushing the vacuum cleaner around the lodger's old room. He brightened up a bit though, when Sugar and Spice explained about the newspaper and Tiger told him what her mum had said.

"Of course you can use the computer," he agreed. "And the fruit and veg really will come in handy. But you'll have to move all this..." he waved his hand at the computer equipment "...somewhere else. I'm going to look for another lodger, so it can't stay here."

That floored us all for a moment. None of us had much space in our houses. Jude and I lived with Mum, and our grandparents. The Oldies had bedrooms, while Jude and I shared the converted attic. We didn't even have enough room for our clothes and stuff, never mind a computer.

"My mum might let us put it in our spare room," Tiger said doubtfully. "But it's full of Dad's drum kit at the moment." Tiger's dad was a drummer with a band.

I turned to Flash. "What about your lean-to?" I asked. The Crumbles had a ramshackle, leaky old conservatory built on to the back of their house.

"OK," Flash agreed, but Cookie shook her head.

"There's no electricity in there," she pointed out.

"Got it!" Jude snapped his fingers. "Our garage is perfect. Grandpa used to have his workshop there, so there's lights and power points and everything. Spex, can you unhook the computer, and we'll move it right away."

I nodded, got down on my knees and began carefully removing cables. Soon we were all loaded up with various bits of equipment and boxes of paper, and we set off for our house in a long line. Mr Hart led the way, carrying the monitor, and I brought up the rear with the printer.

"Hello, hello, hello." Grandpa glanced up from his newspaper as we all filed into our back garden. He and Grandma were sitting out in deck chairs in the shade of the big apple tree. "What are you lot up to now?"

Grandma peered over her silver-rimmed glasses at Sugar and Spice. "Aren't you the new girls from Number Three?" she said with a smile. "Welcome to Cosy Crescent."

"Mr Hart has given us this old computer," Jude said quickly, before the twins could start their "let's confuse everyone" routine. "We're going to start a local newspaper."

"What a splendid idea." Grandpa said smiling at Mr Hart. "That was very kind. Maybe your gran and I could help out."

"Yes, a page for old age pensioners would be a good idea," Gran chimed in.

I couldn't help grinning as Jude looked horrified. But

Tiger nodded. "That's a great idea, Mrs McGee," she said. "We want the newspaper to be for *everybody*."

"Er... sure we do," Jude muttered, pushing open the door of the garage. We all followed him inside, and Grandpa winked at me as I closed the door behind me.

We sometimes hung out in our garage when it was cold and wet outside and we wanted to get out of the house. It was big and airy and, as Jude had pointed out, it had electricity so there was plenty of light and heat. But it was also stuffed with boxes and bags full of things which nobody really wanted but which none of us could bear to throw out. In fact, there was so much junk in there that Mum had given up trying to get the car in and parked it on the drive instead. There were some armchairs lying about which were too shabby even for our living room, and a big, pine kitchen table in the middle which was scratched and worn. We sometimes rigged up a piece of garden netting across the middle and used it for table-tennis matches. But there was nowhere else for the computer to go, so we laid it all out and I began putting it back together.

Jude picked up one of the table-tennis bats and rapped it on the table, making everyone jump. "I reckon we should get down to our first meeting," he said importantly.

"Our first *editorial* meeting," Tiger grinned.

Everyone gathered around the table, perched on stools and slumped into saggy armchairs. I slotted in the last connector and then sat on the arm of Tiger's chair.

"OK, the first thing we need is a name for the newspaper," Jude pointed out. "Any suggestions?"

"The Cosy Crescent Chronicle," said Sugar immediately.

"But we're not just writing about Cosy Crescent, are we?" Cookie pointed out.

"No, of course not," Jude agreed. "It'd be really dull. It's going to be about all of Sunnyvale."

"The Sunnyvale Standard," said Flash dreamily. He might be half-asleep most of the time but sometimes, just sometimes, he'll come up with a really blinding idea!

"Brilliant!" Tiger thumped him on the back, and we all nodded.

"Now." Jude cleared his throat and glanced round the table. "Who's going to be the editor?"

I took my glasses off and pretended to polish them, staring down at the worn surface of the table. I didn't want everyone to guess how much I wanted to be the editor. I really, *really* wanted to do it. But maybe everyone else wanted Jude. Maybe they didn't think I'd be good enough...

"I think Spex should do it," said Tiger casually, winding a strand of hair round and round her finger.

I was so shocked, I nearly dropped my glasses. My head shot up and I stared at Tiger. Jude was staring at her too, looking a bit annoyed.

"Well, *you* don't want to do it, do you, Jude?" Tiger raised her eyebrows at him. "I mean, you don't want to be here, stuck at a desk, when you could be off chasing exciting news stories and doing football reports and stuff, do you?"

"Yeah..." Jude looked thoughtful. He picked the football off the floor, and began to bounce it up and down, frowning.

"And Spex knows all about computers, so he'd be the best person for the job," Tiger said. "After all," she went on, as Jude jumped up and kicked the ball against the opposite wall, "the editor's going to be *sitting down and working at the computer* for hours on end. He won't have time to do much else."

I could see that my brother didn't like the sound of that at all.

"Yeah, Tiger's got a point." Jude nodded. "Is everyone agreed that Spex is editor then?"

There was a murmur of agreement, and Tiger gave me the faintest of winks. Beaming all over my face, I reached for a piece of paper and fished a pen out of my pocket.

"Well, maybe we should start by deciding what kind of things we should put in the paper," I suggested. "If everyone's happy with that—"

"Football reports," Jude jumped in at once. "I could do those." He ran after the football and booted it down

32

to the opposite end of the garage, just missing Flash's head on the way. "And local sports news."

"Sunnyvale news," Tiger broke in. "Events around town like car-boot sales and jumble sales. Oh, and we could have articles about the local carnival and things like that."

"How about a Pet of the Week competition?" Spice said.

"Interviews with famous people who live in Sunnyvale," added Sugar.

"Lots of photos." Flash held up his camera. "We could have some pictures of places to visit around Sunnyvale."

"I've got loads of ideas," Cookie interrupted him. "Competitions, jokes, puzzles, letters page—"

"Hold on, hold on." I was scribbling as fast as I could. "We could have film reviews and book reviews too."

"Don't forget what my mum said," Tiger reminded me. "This isn't just about fun stuff. We can use the paper to say what we think about all kinds of important things."

Cookie frowned. "Are we going to sell the newspaper or give it out for free?" she asked.

Jude tapped the pile of printer paper with his finger. There was so much of it, we'd had to leave some at the Harts' house to collect later. "I think we should give it away until the paper the lodger left behind runs out," he said. "Then we might have to start charging."

"We could put it through people's letter boxes,"

Cookie suggested. "And we could ask Mum to put some in the laundrette." Mrs Crumble did alterations, repairs and ironing for the local laundrette.

"The Post Office where Gran works might let her put some in there," Jude said to me.

"And what about the doctors' surgery where Mum's the receptionist?" I added. "They have loads of magazines and stuff in the waiting room."

"My mum could take some to her yoga class," Tiger chimed in. "And she could take some to the pottery classes she teaches at the local college, too."

"Maybe Mr Kumar will let us put some copies in the shop," Flash suggested. "Then people could take one when they do their shopping." Mr Kumar owned the shop on the corner of Cosy Crescent and Love Lane. It was a newsagent and Post Office too, as well as selling groceries, so lots of people used it.

"Let's go and ask him now." Jude leaped up from his armchair and headed for the door.

"But what about our editorial meeting?" I said, as the others followed him.

"We can carry on talking on the way to the shop," Jude replied impatiently, yanking the door open.

I suppose that, as I was the editor, I should have put my foot down and made everyone stay to finish the meeting, but trying to stop Jude is a bit like trying to stop a hurricane! So I left my notes in a neat pile and ran to catch everyone up. Grandpa and Grandma were dozing in their deck chairs, so we tiptoed through the garden and headed down the crescent towards the shop. As I closed the front gate quietly behind me, Jude nudged me in the ribs.

"It's that guy in the flash car again," he whispered.

I looked round. Guy Lipman was just pulling up at the kerb outside Mrs Dawkins' house.

"Twice in one day!" Tiger wrinkled her nose in surprise. "Mrs D. never has that many visitors."

Guy Lipman waved cheerily at us as he got out of the car and picked up his briefcase. "Hi, kids," he called. "How's things?"

"Great!" Jude beamed at him. "We've just got a computer and we've decided to start our own newspaper."

"What a fantastic idea." Guy Lipman looked really interested. "What are you going to write about?"

"All sorts of things," Tiger told him. "Local issues and stuff."

Guy nodded. "I think that sounds very worthwhile," he began, just as Mrs D.'s front door opened and she peered out, a suspicious look on her wrinkled face. She was still wearing her usual layers of jumpers and cardigans but now she had a huge, fluffy, multi-coloured hat on her head. We were used to her funny hats, but the twins stared at her in amazement and had to put their hands over their mouths to stop their giggles.

"I won't be a minute," Guy called, waving at her.

Mrs Dawkins nodded and went back inside without a word, leaving the front door open. One of her cats, a sleek black one with slanting green eyes, padded outside and sat down on the path to wash herself.

"I'd better go," Guy Lipman shrugged. "I don't like to keep her waiting."

"Is Mrs Dawkins a friend of yours?" Cookie asked innocently.

"Something like that," he replied. "Good luck with your newspaper." And he opened the gate and went into the front garden.

"I wonder what's going on," Tiger said curiously as we watched him walking up the path. "Because something is."

"Are we going to the shop or aren't we?" Jude demanded impatiently.

Everyone moved off down the crescent. I was about to follow them when the cat pushed its way through the bars of the gate and began to wind herself around my ankles. I crouched down on the pavement to stroke her. I liked cats. We'd had one, Benny, until a year ago when he'd got sick and died, and I still missed him.

The tinkle of a mobile phone ringing made me jump.

"Hello?" I could hear Guy Lipman in Mrs Dawkins' front garden. "Yes, yes. I'm here now." There was silence for a moment. "I've told you already," Guy snapped. "I have to keep the old woman sweet until the deal is done. Then we'll be able to do whatever we want."

Chapter Four

I was so shocked, I stayed frozen to the spot. The cat was purring and rubbing its head on my sleeve, but all I could think about was what I'd just heard. Tiger was right. Something was *definitely* going on. The "old woman" Guy had just mentioned had to be Mrs Dawkins But what was the deal he was talking about?

I stayed crouched down on the pavement until I heard Guy Lipman go into the house and shut the door. He couldn't see me crouching down behind the hedge and probably thought we'd all gone off to the shop so it was safe to talk. As soon as I heard the front door slam, I scurried along the crescent, keeping low down until I was well past Mrs Dawkins' house. It was a bit stupid, but I didn't want Guy Lipman to know that I'd overheard what he'd said. Although he'd been very friendly to us, he hadn't sounded friendly on the phone at all.

The others were just coming out of the shop. They were sharing a couple of family-sized bags of crisps, and looking very pleased with themselves. Jude spotted me running towards them and raised his eyebrows.

"Some editor you are, Spex!" he grumbled. "Where did you get to? You were supposed to tell Mr Kumar how completely cool our newspaper is going to be."

"He said yes anyway." Cookie was doing a handstand against the shop wall. She came up for air, then dived into one of the bags and brought out a huge handful of cheese and onion crisps. "He's going to let us put the papers in the shop," she added before stuffing the crisps into her mouth.

"As long as we let him have a free advert," Tiger added. She held out one of the bags to me. "Want a crisp?"

"Never mind that," I gasped. "You'll never believe what I just heard..."

Everyone gathered round me as I quickly told them what had happened.

"I knew something funny was going on!" Tiger said triumphantly.

"Are you sure that's what he said?" Jude asked doubtfully.

I nodded. "Positive."

"I don't get it." Flash frowned. "What kind of deal is he talking about?"

"Maybe we should investigate," Sugar suggested.

"Yes, it might be something we can put in the newspaper!" added Spice eagerly.

Cookie grinned. "We don't have a newspaper yet," she pointed out. "Maybe we should get on with *writing it!*"

"Cookie's right," Jude said sternly. "We've spent too long talking about the paper already. It's time we made a start." He glanced at me. "If that's OK with you, Ed?"

"Sure," I agreed, as we headed back to our house. Whatever was going on with Mrs Dawkins and Guy Lipman, we couldn't let it get in the way of starting up our newspaper.

"Look," Tiger hissed as Mrs D.'s front door opened again. "Here he comes."

We all stopped and stared suspiciously at Guy Lipman as he shook hands with Mrs Dawkins on the doorstep.

"Act normal!" Jude whispered. "We don't want him to know we're on to him."

We all fixed grins to our faces as Guy Lipman strode down the path to his car. He nodded and waved as he jumped in, but luckily he didn't cross the road to speak to us.

"We could go and ask Mrs Dawkins what he's doing

here," Cookie suggested, as the car disappeared round the corner out of the crescent.

"Like she's really going to tell us," Jude scoffed.

"You mean you're scared to ask her," said Tiger with a grin.

"No, I'm not," Jude muttered.

"I'll ask her if you like," Cookie volunteered. "I'm not scared."

"No, Cookie," Flash began, looking alarmed. "I don't think that's a good idea."

But Cookie had already opened the gate and was marching up the path to the front door, humming to herself. I couldn't help feeling a bit impressed. That kid isn't scared of anything!

We all hung around behind the hedge out of sight until we heard Mrs Dawkins open her front door. Then we peered through the leaves to see what was going on.

"Hello, Mrs Dawkins." That was Cookie doing her best butter-wouldn't-melt-in-her-mouth voice. "I was just wondering... who's Mr Lipman?"

Mrs Dawkins scowled at her. "Why do you want to know?"

"Well, he looks like a very important person," Cookie went on innocently, "so we were thinking about interviewing him for our newspaper. We're starting a newspaper, you know." You have to hand it to her, she's smart.

"You'd better ask him yourself," Mrs Dawkins snapped, and shut the door abruptly.

"Good try, Cooks," said Tiger as Cookie cartwheeled down the path to join us again. "But she's not giving anything away, is she?"

"No, but that's a good idea of Cookie's," I said eagerly. "We could ask Guy Lipman if we can interview him for the newspaper. Then we might be able to find out a bit more about what he's planning..."

"How do you spell 'entertaining'?" I muttered to myself, staring at the computer screen. I'm pretty good at spelling, usually, but there was so much noise in our garage, it sounded like the monkey house at the zoo. It was the following morning, and we'd all got together early to start on the first issue of the newspaper. I was sitting at the table, trying to write my editor's welcome bit, which we'd decided would be somewhere on the front page. But I just couldn't concentrate with all that noise going on.

Cookie was sitting next to me, going through a huge joke book and writing down jokes for the puzzle page. The trouble was, she kept reading them out loud and giggling at the answers. "What's red and white and lives under the fridge?" she asked.

I glared at her and stuck my fingers in my ears. Tiger was sitting opposite me. She was designing the

Sunnyvale Standard heading, for the front page, but it didn't seem to be going too well. Every so often she'd mutter under her breath, screw up the piece of paper and chuck it on the floor.

"Oh, and it's another goal from Jude McGee!" Jude roared, slamming the football into the wall just behind my chair and making me jump. That was the second time he'd done that.

"I thought you were supposed to be writing up a report of last week's Sunnyvale Albion match," I groaned.

"I am," Jude said quickly. "But I need to replay the match so that I can remember exactly what happened." He flicked the ball up with his toe and set off down to the other end of the garage. I sighed and bent over the keyboard again.

Over in the corner Flash was talking to Sugar and Spice. Sugar was designing the Pet of the Week page, and Spice was making up some puzzles.

"I need to photograph you now, Spice," Flash explained patiently. He'd been taking photos of us all morning so that we could put our pictures next to our articles. "I've already done Sugar."

"Just use Sugar's photo for me too," said Spice. "No one will be able to tell the difference."

"No, Spex said I had to take photos of everyone," Flash replied doggedly.

"But we look exactly the same!" Spice pouted. "And I want to get on with my puzzles."

I decided to try and take control a bit. After all, I was supposed to be the editor, even if no one ever listened to me! I swivelled round in my chair. "It's OK, Flash," I called. "Why don't you go over to the shop and take a picture of it? Then we can use it in Mr Kumar's free ad."

Flash nodded and wandered out into the crescent. As I turned back to the computer screen, Tiger leaned across the table and handed me a sheet of paper. "What do you think, Spex?"

I stared at the drawing. Tiger had done some great lettering for the name of the paper, with a huge blazing sun rising above the words. "It's great," I said eagerly. "Come and have a look, everyone."

The others crowded round. They all liked it as much as I did, and now that we finally had our newspaper heading, everyone seemed to get stuck into their work much faster. Jude stopped kicking the football around and sat down to write for a couple of minutes, and Tiger nicked Cookie's joke book and sat on it, so at last there was peace and quiet in the garage... for about two minutes! Suddenly Flash burst through the door, moving faster than I'd ever seen him move before.

"That Lipman's back!" he panted.

Immediately we all jumped up and ran for the door. Guy Lipman's expensive car was once again parked outside Mrs Dawkins' house. The boot was open, and he was lifting some heavy-looking boxes out of it.

"I don't know what this deal he's got going is all about," Jude said in a low voice, "But it must be something big. He's coming to see Mrs D. every single day."

"We're going to ask him if he'll do an interview for the paper, right?" Tiger whispered. "Then maybe we can find out a bit more."

"Let me do it," said Jude and he hurried across the road before we could stop him.

"Quick, you lot!" Tiger shook her hair off her face and rushed after him. "Before he puts his foot right in it!"

Guy Lipman was struggling with two heavy boxes, and trying to hold his smart silver briefcase under his arm at the same time.

"Hi," Jude said politely. "Can I give you a hand?"

"Thanks." Guy allowed Jude to take the briefcase while we all watched. Suddenly Tiger nudged me.

"Do you see what's in the boxes?" she whispered.

I squinted at the writing on the side. *PerfectPaw Gourmet Cat Food*. The most expensive cat food in the supermarket. We'd only ever bought that for Benny at Christmas, and Guy Lipman had two huge boxfuls of it!

45

"He's trying to butter Mrs Dawkins up by buying her expensive stuff for her cats," I muttered.

Guy Lipman was making his way up the path, staggering a little under the weight of the boxes. Jude followed, lugging the briefcase which seemed almost as heavy.

"Er, Mr Lipman," he began, "We were wondering if you'd mind being interviewed for our newspaper—"

Jude didn't get any further. Suddenly the briefcase burst open. It was packed with papers and files, and they spilled out on to the path in a big heap. Guy Lipman looked furious.

"Sorry," Jude gabbled, sweeping the papers into his arms. "It wasn't my fault, it just came open."

The front door opened and Mrs Dawkins looked out. Immediately Guy Lipman thrust the boxes inside and hurried back down the path towards Jude. "Leave them," he snapped. "I'll do it."

"Sorry." Jude backed away. He hurried out of the garden and across the road towards us.

"What's up?" I asked curiously. He looked like he'd had a major shock.

"I saw some papers when they fell out of the briefcase," Jude said in a low voice. "They were plans. It looks as though Guy Lipman is trying to buy the fields around Cosy Crescent from Mrs Dawkins, and I think he is planning to build a huge supermarket there!"

Chapter Five

I was so shocked I couldn't say anything. The Cosy Crescent fields where I'd played almost all of my life, dug up and concreted over? A supermarket instead of green grass and a lake and woodland and lots of wildlife?

I glanced round at the others. They all looked as shocked as I was.

"Mr Lipman can't do that!" Tiger gasped.

"He's got the plans," replied Jude grimly. "And I don't think he'd be trying to buy the fields if there wasn't a chance he could get the supermarket built."

"But those fields are *everybody's*," Flash said in a bewildered voice. "I mean, I know they really belong to Mrs Dawkins, but everyone in Sunnyvale uses them. Dad takes me fishing at the lake when he's not working."

"My class goes there all the time," Cookie said, her lip quivering . "We're doing a project about squirrels."

"It won't be quiet around here any more, will it?" said Sugar sadly.

"If there's a supermarket there'll be lots of people," Spice added. "And cars."

"We can't let him get away with this!" Tiger declared, hands on her hips. "Come on." And she marched across the road towards Mrs D.'s house. "We have to find out if she's going to sell the fields or not."

"Wait!" I hurried after her. "Is this a good idea?"

Tiger spun round and glared at me. She's normally pretty even-tempered, but when she gets mad, she gets mad.

"OK, it's a good idea," I said quickly, adjusting my glasses. "But I think we ought to wait until Guy Lipman's gone before we speak to Mrs Dawkins."

"All right," agreed Tiger reluctantly.

"Let's go back and carry on with the newspaper then," Flash suggested.

We all trailed back to the garage in silence. Jude offered to be the lookout and hang around outside, watching for Guy Lipman to leave, so we left him on the corner kicking the football around and trying to look innocent.

I sat down in front of the computer and tried to concentrate on my editorial, but I couldn't. All I could

48

think about was what would happen if the fields disappeared. They'd been there all my life and I was so used to them, I hardly thought about them any more. They were just *there*. But maybe they wouldn't be there for much longer, if Guy Lipman had his way. The thought made my insides turn over.

We were all quiet but no one was really doing anything much. We were all listening for Jude. Then, about five minutes later, we heard him come thundering down the path towards the garage. "He's gone!" he panted, sticking his head round the door.

"Who's going to do the talking?" I asked as we filed across the road towards Mrs Dawkins' house.

"I will," Tiger broke in as Jude opened his mouth. She'd calmed down a bit by now, but she still had a glint in her eye that could mean trouble.

"But—" Jude began.

Tiger whipped round, her hair flying. "All right?" she asked, eyeballing Jude.

"Absolutely," Jude agreed quickly.

Tiger rang the door bell, and we waited in silence. Sometimes Mrs D. wouldn't open the door at all, depending on how she was feeling. Although I wasn't really *scared* of her, she could be a bit frightening if she was in a bad mood. The twins were looking nervous, especially Sugar, who was keeping out of sight behind Jude. And Flash was messing about with his camera, like he always did when he was a bit wound up.

Suddenly the door flew open without warning, and we all nearly jumped out of our skins. Sugar gasped and clutched Spice's arm, and even Jude looked a bit alarmed.

Mrs Dawkins stood on the doorstep glaring at us. "What do you want?" she asked abruptly.

Tiger squared her shoulders. "It's about Mr Lipman," she said, staring Mrs Dawkins straight in the eye. "Is it true you're selling the Cosy Crescent fields to him?"

Mrs Dawkins didn't bat an eyelid. "Is that any of your business?" she wanted to know.

"Yes, because we live here," Tiger argued. "We don't want the fields to be built on."

Mrs Dawkins looked pretty angry. Sugar peeped out from behind Jude's back and hastily popped out of sight again. My knees felt a bit wobbly and even Cookie was looking worried. "Well, you kids should be grateful," she said sharply. "Mr Lipman's got great plans for the fields. This town really needs a community hall. The hall, a children's playground and an animal sanctuary won't take up much space, and most of the fields will still be there." And she slammed the door shut in our faces.

"What does she mean, a community hall, a playground and an animal sanctuary?" Jude asked, looking puzzled. "There was none of those things on the plans. Just a huge supermarket with a massive car park."

"It's obvious, isn't it?" Tiger said impatiently. "That's what Lipman's *told* Mrs Dawkins he's going to do."

"To get her to sell the fields, you mean?" Flash wanted to know.

"Yes, Brains." Jude slapped Flash on the back.

"We've got to tell her the truth," Tiger said determinedly, reaching for the door bell.

"She won't listen," said Cookie immediately. "You know what she's like."

Flash looked miserable. "So there's nothing we can do."

"Oh, yes, there is!"

Everyone turned to stare at me, as I had called out so loudly. OK, I'm not usually *quite* so loud, but I couldn't believe that everyone was going to give up without a fight.

"What do you mean?" asked Jude.

"We've got the newspaper, haven't we?" I pointed out. "We can start a campaign to stop Guy Lipman building a supermarket on our fields!"

"Flash, where's that photo of Guy Lipman standing next to his car?"

"Here." Flash hurried over to me, the photo in his hand.

"Great." I took it and positioned it carefully on the mocked-up copy of our very first front page. Above the photo was a big, black headline which read:

What Does Mr Lipman Really Want with the Cosy Crescent Fields?

I grinned, gave Flash a thumbs up and then turned to look at the others. Since I'd reminded everyone that we could use the newspaper to try and stop Guy Lipman, all the messing about and time wasting had stopped. Everyone was working really hard to try and get their articles finished so that we could get the paper out as fast as possible. Even Jude had managed to sit still for five minutes to finish his football report without having to be tied down!

Sugar and Spice were sitting in the corner finishing off the puzzles page, their heads bent over the same piece of paper. Meanwhile Tiger and Cookie were at the printer, sorting out some of the pages that were ready, but we still had quite a lot to do. It was lucky we hadn't set a deadline for the first issue. Although I thought we ought to get the paper out as soon as we could, then everyone would find out exactly what Guy Lipman was up to.

"When do you think we should tell our parents what's going on?" I asked, adjusting the headline so it was perfectly centred. We'd decided not to say anything to anyone yet. Tiger had pointed out that we didn't have any proof, except for what Jude had seen. We were hoping that maybe something else would turn up to back up our story before the first issue came out.

Tiger cleared her throat. "Well, I did kind of mention it to Mum yesterday," she admitted.

"And Sugar told Dad," Spice chimed in.

"I didn't," said Sugar indignantly. "*You* did!"

Flash was looking a bit sheepish too.

"He forgot we weren't supposed to tell Mum," Cookie said, leaping to her brother's defence.

I rolled my eyes. "So Jude and I are the only ones who kept quiet?"

"Er, actually…" Jude began.

I groaned.

"I did say something to Gramps," he went on.

"What did he say?" I asked.

Jude looked a bit embarrassed. "He thought that maybe we'd made a mistake," he replied.

"You mean that *you* might have made a mistake," Tiger grinned.

"I know what I saw on those plans," Jude said doggedly.

"Mum said we must have got it wrong too," Cookie put in. "She said that Mrs Dawkins would never sell the fields if a supermarket was going to be built there."

"Dad was quite pleased," said Spice.

"He thinks he might be able to get a job in the supermarket," added Sugar.

"My mum didn't believe it either," Tiger admitted. "But she said Jude's grandad was going to speak to Mrs Dawkins."

"Flash, where are you going?" I asked. He was wandering over to the door, looking dreamy.

"Sorry?" Flash jumped and turned round. "I'm going to take some pictures of the fields. You know, to use in the newspaper."

"Let's all go." Jude jumped up eagerly. "We've been stuck in here for hours. It's like being at school!"

We all trooped out of the garage into the hot sunshine. The sky was blue and cloudless, and usually we'd have been outside kicking a football around or going to the local swimming pool or for a picnic in the countryside. But not any more. The newspaper was too important.

"Hello, kids." Grandpa was pottering around the garden. He pulled a red handkerchief out of his waistcoat pocket and wiped his forehead. "Phew! It's too warm for gardening."

"Gramps, have you spoken to Mrs Dawkins about the fields?" Jude wanted to know.

Grandpa nodded. "You don't need to worry," he said kindly. "Mrs Dawkins told me exactly what Guy Lipman's planning. It's about time we had a community hall."

"But the plans—" Jude began.

"I mentioned that," Grandpa went on. "Mrs Dawkins says you must be mistaken."

"I wasn't," Jude muttered as we headed out of our garden.

"We know that," I said loyally.

As we walked down the crescent, Mrs D. opened her front door to let one of her cats out. She glanced crossly at us and went back inside without a word.

"She's mad at us," Cookie whispered as Jude opened the gate to the fields.

"You know what she's like," Tiger replied. "She gets an idea into her head and she sticks to it. She's decided Guy Lipman's nice, and we're the bad guys."

A cool breeze was blowing across the fields from the lake. There were groups of people picnicking on the grass, and fishing in the lake. Everything looked fresh and green. As Flash lifted his camera and began to click away, nobody said anything. But I guessed that they were all thinking the same thing as I was.

There was no way we could let Guy Lipman build a supermarket here.

"I don't like this." Tiger frowned at the rest of us. It was four days later, and we were sitting round the table in our garage, working on the paper. "Guy Lipman hasn't been here at all for the last few days. What's going on?"

"Maybe nothing's going on." Jude tilted his chair back. He'd been sitting still for ten minutes and I could see that he was now getting bored! "Maybe he's given up."

"No way." Tiger shook her head, her long hair flying. "People like him don't give up."

"Mrs D.'s been in a bad mood," an upside-down Cookie chimed in. She was doing a handstand against the garage wall. She claimed that being upside-down made her think better. "She hasn't come out of her house for ages."

"I know," said Tiger. "Mum went over to see if she was OK, and she wouldn't open the door."

"What are we going to do about the newspaper?" I asked. "Are we still going to go with the front page or what?"

Tiger wound a strand of hair round her finger. "We'd better wait until we find out if the sale's going ahead or not," she said slowly.

Jude yawned. "I've got an idea."

"What?" I wanted to know.

"Ice-cream break!" Jude grinned. He kicked his chair away and sauntered out of the garage, hands in his jeans pockets. Flash, Cookie, Sugar and Spice immediately followed him.

I sighed and looked round at the table which was stacked with bits of paper.

"Come on, Spex." Tiger patted me on the back. "An ice-cream break won't hurt. And Jude has sat still for ten minutes – that's got to be a record!"

Grinning, I followed her outside and we caught up with the others. But we forgot all about ice creams when we saw Guy Lipman's car parked alongside the kerb.

"He's back!" Cookie whispered.

We edged our way across the road towards the car, trying to look innocent, although we must have looked pretty suspicious! Because it was another baking hot day, Mr Lipman had left his windows down.

"Look!" Jude pointed inside the car. The silver briefcase lay on the back seat. "I wonder if the plans are inside?"

"Don't even think about it," Tiger broke in sternly. "You're not going to have a look."

"I'd be really quick," Jude replied, resting his hands on the open window. "Nobody would know—"

"Hey!" An angry shout from behind us made everyone jump. "What are you kids doing?"

Chapter Six

We hadn't noticed Mrs D.'s front door open. Guy Lipman was striding down the garden path towards us. He looked rather annoyed, but was trying not to show it. Mrs Dawkins hovered in the doorway, wearing a hat that looked like a tea cosy. She didn't look too pleased either.

"We're not doing anything," Jude said quickly, stepping back from the car.

Mr Lipman bent down to check on the briefcase in the back seat. Then he forced a smile. "Sorry," he said, pulling a dazzling white handkerchief from his pocket and mopping his brow. "I knew you weren't up to anything really. It's this weather. It can make you a bit hot and bothered."

We watched in silence as he waved to Mrs D., got into the car, and sped off. She waited until he'd disappeared round the corner of the crescent, then gave us a glare and went inside, slamming the door as usual. It was so obvious that we were not her favourite people at the moment.

"So the sale must still be going ahead," Tiger said, sounding frustrated. "We've *got* to finish the newspaper and let people know what's going on."

"It's a shame we can't find out a bit more about Lipman," I said thoughtfully. "Then we might be able to get some more proof about what he's up to."

"We could ask Mrs Dawkins," suggested Flash dozily. Then he blushed as we all gave him a *look*. "Bad idea. Sorry."

"Sugar's scared of her," Spice grinned.

"I am not!" muttered Sugar.

"Well, I've got another idea," Cookie said brightly.

We all turned to look at her.

"What?" asked Jude.

"This." Cookie pointed at the pavement. For a minute I thought she'd gone mad! But there, on the ground, was a small, white card with words printed in blue.

"It must have fallen out of Mr Lipman's pocket when he pulled his hanky out," Cookie explained. "I only just noticed it."

Tiger was the first to kneel down and pick it up. "It's

a business card," she exclaimed, showing it to the rest of us. *Meadowbank Property Developers* was printed on it along with telephone and fax numbers and an email address. "I wonder if it's the name of Mr Lipman's company."

"It could be a card someone else has given him," I pointed out, as we all stared at it. It wasn't much, but maybe it would give us a start.

"Hi, kids." Mrs Cubb was walking towards Sugar and Spice's house. She was carrying a basket of vegetables on her arm. It was stuffed with tomatoes and onions, potatoes and courgettes. "What are you up to?"

Tiger held out the business card. "Mum, have you ever heard of these people?" she asked.

Mrs Cubb squinted at the card in the sunshine. "Hmm, the name *does* sound familiar," she said slowly. "I'll ask around."

"Are those for us?" Spice asked, peering into the basket.

"They look nice," added Sugar.

Mrs Cubb frowned. "Now which one of you is which?"

"I'm Sugar," began Spice.

"Don't start that again!" Jude groaned. "Come on, let's get those ice creams."

Mrs Cubb went over to Number Three, while we headed down the crescent to the shop. Jude and Tiger went in to buy the ice creams while the rest of us hung around outside.

"Right," I said firmly, as soon as everyone had a cone in their hands. "Let's go straight back to the garage and get on with the paper."

Nobody grumbled or complained. Seeing Mr Lipman again had reminded everyone what we were up against and why we were working so hard on our newspaper. We all marched back to our garage and got to work.

There were still a few articles and pages to finish. Jude had interviewed Mr Queen, who manages Sunnyvale Albion. It would be the first in our series of interviews with local celebrities, and Jude was still working on it. Sugar and Spice were finishing off their Pet of the Week page. Flash had taken a photo of Mr Kumar's Jack Russell terrier, Max, and the twins had decided to make him their first featured pet. They'd even written an "interview" with Max, as if the dog was speaking to them, which was pretty funny! Meanwhile, Cookie and Tiger were at the printer again, churning out page after page after page.

"The scanner's not working properly," Flash said suddenly. He was trying to scan the photo of Max on to the computer.

"It's a bit slow," I replied. "Give it time."

"No, there's something wrong," Flash insisted.

I put down the pages I was stapling together, and went over to take a look. I was checking the machine, when Tiger and Cookie both groaned.

"Spex, the printer's jammed," Tiger called anxiously.

Muttering under my breath, I sprinted over to them. A wad of paper had got caught inside, and the red alarm button was flashing.

"Try to pull it out gently without tearing it," I told her.

Tiger did her best, but the paper ripped, leaving half of it still stuck.

"We'll have to get Grandpa to open the printer up," I groaned. Suddenly it seemed as if everything was going wrong at once.

"Did I hear someone mention my name?" Grandpa enquired. He had just put his head round the door.

"Hey, Gramps," I said thankfully. "Could you open the printer for us? There's some paper stuck inside."

"Sure." Grandpa ambled over to his workbench and picked up a screwdriver. "By the way, I've just been talking to Mrs Dawkins. She told me that the sale of the fields is going ahead. She's signing the contract on Saturday."

Everyone gasped.

"Saturday!" I repeated despairingly. That was only three days away. We had to get the newspaper finished, printed *and* give it out to people in just *three days*. I turned to the others. "We'll have to get the newspaper finished tomorrow," I told them.

Everyone groaned.

"But that only gives us two days to give them out to everyone," Tiger pointed out. "Will that be long enough?"

"It'll have to be," I said in a determined voice.

Chapter Seven

We had to go for it. There was no other way. We sat in the garage all day while the sun blazed outside, working our socks off to try and get everything finished. Luckily Gramps managed to unblock the printer, but it took me ages to figure out what was wrong with the scanner. By the time I'd fixed it, it was too late to do any more scanning. Our parents were starting to get annoyed too. Mrs Crumble came over to collect Flash and Cookie, and Mr Hart turned up to take the twins home. Tiger stayed on as late as she could, but eventually she had to go too. Jude and I worked on, but when Mum came out for the fifth time to tell us that dinner was ready, we could see that she was getting mad! So we gave up and went inside.

"I've got a great idea," Jude whispered as we all sat watching TV after dinner. "We'll sneak into the garage when everyone's gone to bed, and carry on working."

A great idea? It was a completely stupid idea! We didn't even make it to the bottom of the stairs. Grandpa heard us tiptoeing around and thought we were burglars. He was about to call the police before he realised that it was us! We were marched back to bed and told to stay put until the morning.

Next day Jude and I were up as soon as it was light. We didn't even stop for breakfast. By seven thirty we were in the garage, printing page after page of the newspaper.

"I hope the others get here soon," I said anxiously, glancing at the clock. It was going to be a real race against time to get everything finished.

"Hi." The outside door opened and Tiger stuck her head round it. "Need any help?"

"You bet," I said gratefully. "Any sign of the others?"

Tiger swung the door open wider. The twins and Cookie were behind her.

"Excellent." Jude grinned. He thrust a pile of pages into Tiger's hands. "Come on, get stapling!"

"Where's Flash?" I asked Cookie.

She shrugged. "He'll be here in a minute."

We all helped to lay out piles of paper on the table. All of the pages of the newspaper were finished, but now we had the enormous job of putting all the sheets together in order. Tiger suggested a kind of conveyor-belt system where we all walked round the table picking up sheet after sheet and then stapling them together at the end. It worked pretty well, and the pile of finished copies began to grow bigger and bigger.

"Sorry I'm late." Yawning, Flash wandered into the garage. I stared at him. His hair was sticking up, but that wasn't why I was staring.

"Hey, Flash," I said. "Isn't that your pyjama top you're wearing?"

"What?" Flash looked down at his blue and white striped top. "Oh. I forgot to change."

We all burst out laughing.

"At least you remembered to take your pyjama trousers off and put your jeans on," Tiger said. She handed him the stapler. "You can sit at the end of the table and staple the sheets together when we've collected them."

"Maybe you should do a fashion page in the next issue, Flash," Jude suggested with a grin.

We carried on working. It was pretty boring just walking around the table picking up sheet after sheet and handing them to Flash to be stapled, but watching the pile of newspapers growing and growing made us keep going. Grandpa and Grandma brought us a big tray of orange juice and toast, which kept us going too, although we had to be careful not to get any buttery crumbs on the newspapers!

It was getting close to lunch time by the time we'd almost finished.

"The very last copy!" announced Tiger, looking down at the table. Only one page of each sheet of the newspaper remained.

"It's a bit special," said Cookie. "Who gets to do this one?"

"Spex," Sugar and Spice said together.

"Yes," agreed Tiger. "He's the one who's kept us at it. If it wasn't for him, we'd never have finished."

I looked at my feet, feeling very embarrassed. I took off my glasses and pretended to clean them, so that I didn't have to look at everyone.

"Go on, Spex," Jude urged.

Solemnly I picked up the last sheets of the very last copy of the newspaper. Everyone cheered as I handed them to Flash and he stapled them together.

"Hurray!" Sugar and Spice said at exactly the same moment, and they both collapsed into the same armchair, looking exhausted.

"No time for that," Tiger said briskly, hauling them both to their feet. "We need to start handing them out."

"Let's take a whole load of them down to the corner shop now," Jude suggested.

We gathered a big pile of newspapers for Mr Kumar. Then we found some empty cardboard boxes and stacked the rest of the papers inside. To keep them flat and clean we piled some old glossy magazines on top, which had been dumped in a corner of the garage. Then we each took a wodge of newspapers and set off.

As usual, we checked to see if Mr Lipman's car was outside Mrs D.'s house. It wasn't. But there *was* a car parked outside the Cubbs' house that we'd never seen before. And I think I'd have remembered it if we had! It was old and rusty and painted bright pink.

"I wonder who that belongs to?" Tiger said with a frown.

We didn't have to wait long to find out. As we walked past the Cubbs' house, the front door opened and Tiger's mum looked out.

"Wait a minute, kids," she called. "There's someone here I'd like you to meet."

We stopped as Mrs Cubb came outside, followed by another woman. I blinked. Her hair was almost exactly the same colour pink as the car! She had a big golden greyhound on a leash who padded along beside her.

"Oh, he's lovely!" said Tiger. She shoved her newspapers into Jude's arms and knelt down to stroke the dog. Although he was so big, he seemed very gentle.

"This is my friend, Lynn," Mrs Cubb explained. "She

lives quite a way from Sunnyvale, but she's come over especially to talk to you."

Lynn smiled at us. "I'm really pleased to meet you," she said. She looked at the pile of newspapers in my arms and reached over to take one. "Willow asked me if I knew anything about the Meadowbank Property Company and, as it happens, I know quite a bit about Mr Guy Lipman."

"You do?" Jude asked eagerly.

Lynn nodded. "He owns Meadowbank," she said, "and not long ago his company bought some land in the town where I live. He wanted to build new houses, but to do so, he had to close down a big animal sanctuary." She frowned, looking very angry for a moment. "He gave the sanctuary hardly any notice. They thought they'd have to put some of the animals down but luckily they managed to rehome them all in time." She patted the greyhound who was gently licking Tiger's nose. "That's where I got Billy from."

"But how can he do things like that?" Cookie asked.

Lynn shrugged. "I don't know for sure, but I think he has some very important friends in high places," she said. "I wouldn't be at all surprised if he does plan to build a supermarket on your fields."

"It looks like you kids were right and everyone else was wrong," Mrs Cubb sighed. "And I'm quite sure Mrs Dawkins doesn't realise what's going on."

"We've got to tell her then!" Tiger gave Billy a final pat and jumped to her feet. "Mrs D. loves animals. She wouldn't be happy at all if she knew what Mr Lipman had done."

"Maybe Lynn should come with you," Mrs Cubb suggested. "She might listen to her."

"I'll be glad to," Lynn agreed.

"Let's go now," Tiger said.

A car horn beeping made us all turn round. It was Mum on her way to work. We waved at her and then headed off to Mrs Dawkins'.

As we walked up Mrs D.'s garden path, I began to feel more hopeful that we could stop her from selling the fields to Mr Lipman. Surely she wouldn't want to go ahead when she heard what Lynn had to say?

But it was the same old story. Although Tiger rang the door bell several times, Mrs Dawkins wouldn't open the door.

"Why don't we put one of the newspapers through the letter box?" Cookie suggested. "She'd have to read it then."

"No, wait." Tiger frowned, thinking hard. "I think we ought to add a stop-press bit, about what Lynn has told us. We can easily staple it on to the end of all the copies of the paper. And it won't take long to write."

"Great idea," Sugar and Spice said together.

"Thanks for coming, Lynn," Tiger said gratefully, and we all nodded.

"Good luck," Lynn called after us as we hurried back to the garage.

"I'll write up what Lynn told us," I said, pushing open the door. "Tiger and Cookie, you can print off the copies, and the others can add it to the newspapers."

"OK," said Jude, looking a bit dazed. "But where *are* the newspapers?"

I stared across the garage. The cardboard boxes which held the papers had vanished.

Chapter Eight

I blinked. I couldn't believe my eyes.

"Where *are* they?" I gasped.

Tiger rushed across the garage, her hair flying behind her. "They must be here *somewhere*," she said anxiously. "Quick, start looking."

We started hunting desperately through all the rubbish in the garage. We moved aside boxes of Christmas decorations, piles of old books, bags of clothes ready for the Scouts' jumble sale and loads of other stuff. But the newspapers were nowhere to be found.

"Hang on a minute." Jude clicked his fingers. "I've got it!"

"What?" we all said together.

"I bet Mr Lipman's found out about the newspaper,"

Jude said triumphantly. "He's stolen them!"

Tiger shook her head. "That's daft," she said firmly. "How would he have known where they were?"

"Or what we've put in it?" added Cookie.

I frowned. "I wonder if someone's moved them," I said, just as Grandpa popped his head round the garage door.

"Lunch is ready, kids," he called.

"Gramps, our newspapers have gone!" Jude said urgently. "Have you moved them?"

Grandpa shook his head. "No, son, of course not," he replied. "No one's been in here all morning except you. Oh, and your mother."

"Mum?" I remembered how we'd seen Mum driving off to do the afternoon shift at the surgery. "What was she doing in here?"

"She was going to stop off at the shopping centre on the way to work, so she decided to take all the recycling as well," replied Grandpa. "You know the recycling centre is right next to the shops."

"Recycling!" Tiger repeated, looking a bit pale.

"Grandpa, did you see what she put in the car?" I asked quickly.

"Oh, yes." Grandpa nodded. "Cardboard boxes full of glass bottles and jars. Oh, and magazines too."

"Our newspapers!" Cookie cried despairingly. "Mrs McGee's taken them to be recycled!"

"We've got to stop her," Jude gasped. "If she tips the boxes into the recycling bin, we'll never get the newspapers back."

"Quick!" Tiger yelled, rushing over to the door. "We'll have to run. Mrs McGee went ages ago."

Mrs Cubb was standing at the kerb waving to Lynn as she drove off. She saw us charging down our drive and raised her eyebrows.

"What on earth is the matter?" she called.

Breathlessly Tiger explained. "And we've got to get the newspapers back or we won't be able to tell everyone what Mr Lipman's up to!" she finished.

"I'll take you in the van," Mrs Cubb replied immediately.

The Cubbs' camper van was parked in their drive. It was pretty old but it was painted all over with bright swirls of pink, purple and silver which hid the rust patches. Mrs Cubb fetched the keys and we all jumped in.

"Hurry, Mum," Tiger urged.

Mrs Cubb turned the key in the ignition. There was a splutter, and then the engine died away.

"Oh no!" Jude groaned.

"Sometimes Petunia takes a little time to get going," explained Mrs Cubb, turning the key again.

"Petunia?" Sugar and Spice giggled.

We all sat there impatiently as Mrs Cubb tried to get Petunia going. Then, all of a sudden, the engine stuttered into life. It was the most wonderful sound I've ever heard!

"Here we go!" said Mrs Cubb, pulling the van off the driveway.

I was on the edge of my seat as Tiger's mum drove down Cosy Crescent and turned into Love Lane. Would we get there in time to stop Mum recycling our newspapers? Or would all our hard work have been for nothing? And more importantly, how were we going to stop Guy Lipman and his plans for the fields without our newspaper?

"The traffic is terrible," said Mrs Cubb, tapping her fingers on the steering wheel as we joined a long queue of cars.

"So are these seats," Jude whispered in my ear. I grinned as he half stood up and showed me the spring that was sticking out of his seat.

"Hurry, Mum!" Tiger said again, as we finally left most of the traffic behind and got closer to the shopping centre.

"Petunia's doing her best," Mrs Cubb replied. She indicated right to turn into the road that led to the shopping centre. As she turned the wheel, Petunia gave a sort of cough. The van shuddered a bit, shaking us in our seats. And then the engine cut out completely.

"Oh no!" Mrs Cubb groaned. "What's happened?"

"Quick!" Tiger, who was in the front seat next to her mum, flung the door open. "We'll have to run the rest of the way!"

We all jumped out and ran, leaving poor Mrs Cubb to call the breakdown people. Jude and Tiger were the fastest, and they left me and the others panting along behind them. We caught up with them as they stood at the gates of the recycling centre, trying to spot Mum's car. It was packed with people and there were long queues at all the recycling banks.

"What if..." Spice began.

"...she's already come and recycled, and gone away again?" Sugar finished off.

I had an awful, cold feeling of dread right in the middle of my tummy. But suddenly my heart leaped.

"There she is!" I yelled.

Mum's car was parked in a long queue for the paper banks. As we threaded our way through the cars towards her, she pulled up to the huge recycling bins and got out to open the boot.

"Mum!" Jude shouted, waving his arms above his head like a windmill. "Don't do it!"

Mum stared at us and blinked behind her gold-rimmed glasses as if she couldn't believe her eyes. "What on earth are you lot doing here?" she asked, bewildered.

Jude and Tiger had dived into the open boot and

were rummaging around under the magazines in the cardboard boxes.

"They're here!" Tiger called triumphantly, holding up a handful of newspapers.

We all cheered. But Mum looked shocked as she realised what she'd *almost* done.

"Don't worry," Jude said, giving her a big hug. "We've got them back, and that's all that matters."

"Well, I think I'd better take you *and* your newspapers home," Mum said, looking very relieved.

"Won't you be late for work?" I asked.

Mum glanced at her watch. "No, I've got time," she said. "I can leave the shopping until tonight."

It was a bit of a squeeze for us all to get into the car, but we managed it with Cookie sitting on Tiger's lap. I climbed in next to Flash, grinning all over my face. I couldn't stop smiling. Things had so nearly gone horribly wrong, but now Operation Guy Lipman was back on again!

"Would you like a copy of our newspaper?" Cookie politely asked a young mum who was pushing a pram. "It's really good, you know."

The woman laughed. "OK," she said. She took it and was about to roll it up and pop it in her shopping bag when she caught sight of the front page. *What does Mr Lipman Really Want with the Cosy Crescent Fields?*

Frowning, she skimmed through the article.

"That's terrible," she said a moment later. "Really terrible. Well done for bringing it to people's attention."

We all beamed at her. It was the day after Mum had tried to recycle our newspapers, and we were standing on the corner of Cosy Crescent and Love Lane, handing them out to passers-by. We'd worked hard all of yesterday afternoon to add in the extra information that Lynn had given us, and then we'd started on the job of getting the papers out to as many people in Sunnyvale as we could. Mr Kumar had a huge stack of them in the shop, and Sugar and Spice kept popping in to see how many had gone. Lots and lots, they told us gleefully.

Mum had taken a stack for the doctors' waiting room, Gran had taken a big pile for the Post Office and Mrs Crumble had put some in the laundrette. Tiger's mum and dad were giving them out to everyone they met, and Jude had asked Mr Queen, the football manager, to give some out too. We'd already got rid of over half of them.

"I put one through Mrs D.'s letter box this morning," Tiger remarked, handing a paper to an elderly man as he shuffled past. "I just hope she's read it."

"There are loads of people on the fields today." Cookie shaded her eyes from the blazing sun and looked down the crescent. "Maybe we should go and hand out some papers over there?"

"Good idea," Jude agreed. "Spex? You, Flash and Cookie can go."

"OK." I scooped up some extra newspapers from the pile on the pavement. Flash and Cookie did the same.

"Let's see if we can get rid of them all today," Jude said a bit bossily, and Tiger winked at me.

"Let's have a race," Cookie suggested. "Bet you that Flash, Spex and I can get rid of all our papers before you do."

"You're on!" Jude agreed.

I laughed as Cookie, Flash and I made our way down the crescent towards the fields with our armfuls of papers.

"You've done it now, Cooks," I said. "You know Jude – he hates to lose!"

Cookie grinned. "I don't care who wins," she replied, "As long as we hand out *all* of the papers!"

The fields were full of people sunbathing, picnicking, fishing, playing football and rambling through the woods. We started giving the newspapers away and everyone was really interested.

"What can we do to help?" asked one man, who was having a picnic with his two children.

"Well, we may not be in time to stop the fields from being sold tomorrow," I explained. "But we can start up a campaign to stop a supermarket being built."

Cookie nudged me. "Do you really think we're too late to stop Mrs Dawkins?" she asked.

"Yes, she must have read the newspaper by now," added Flash.

"Or she might have screwed it up and put it in the bin without looking at it," I pointed out with a sigh.

Cookie ran off across the grass and handed a copy of the newspaper to a woman walking her dog. "That's the last one!" she announced triumphantly.

"Let's go and see how Jude and the others are getting on," I said. So we made our way back across the fields to the corner of Cosy Crescent. The others had done well too. Tiger was holding the last couple of copies in her hand.

"We beat you!" Cookie laughed, as Tiger gave them out to two people walking past.

"We did it!" Sugar and Spice crowed together. "We haven't got a single paper left!"

We all cheered. Although we were hot and tired, it was worth it. We'd made sure that lots of people knew what was going on. Now all we had to do was wait and see what happened tomorrow.

"We'll have to be up bright and early," said Tiger in a determined voice, as we walked up the crescent. "We must try and speak to Mrs Dawkins before Guy Lipman arrives with the contract, and find out if she's read the newspaper or not. Then we might just have a chance of changing her mind."

"OK," said Spice.

We'll meet out here in the crescent tomorrow morning," said Tiger. "And remember, make it early."

"Anything happening yet?" Jude asked as he and I made our way over to Tiger. It was the following morning, and she was standing outside Mrs Dawkins' house.

"No, but Mrs Dawkins is definitely up," Tiger replied. "She's looked out of the window once or twice. I reckon she's waiting for Guy Lipman to arrive."

"Hi!" Sugar and Spice called, running across the road towards us. Sugar was yawning and Spice was still tying a ribbon in her hair. "Did we miss anything?"

"Not yet," I replied. A few seconds later, Cookie and Flash appeared from Number Four. Cookie was wide-awake but Flash looked half-asleep and had a piece of toast in his hand. He was staring at it as if he had no idea how it had got there.

"Where did that come from?" he asked.

"I gave it to you," Cookie told him. "You got up so late, you didn't have time for any breakfast."

"Oh." Flash took a big bite, dropping crumbs down his sweatshirt.

"Right, let's go and see Mrs D.," Tiger announced, a glint in her eyes. But as she turned to open the gate, the roar of an engine behind us made us all jump.

Guy Lipman's car raced up the crescent and screeched to a halt outside Mrs Dawkins' house. Next moment he jumped out and strode over to us. He was red in the face and in his hand he was clutching a copy of our newspaper.

"Do you mind telling me what *this* is all about?" he snapped.

Chapter Nine

For some reason I didn't feel scared at all. It was our newspaper, and it was good, and I was going to stand up for it!

"That's our newspaper," I said firmly. "We told you we were starting one."

Jude's mouth fell open and he stared at me. So did the others. OK, I don't speak up very often, but I *was* the editor, after all!

"I've got no problem with that," Mr Lipman snarled. "But what I do have a problem with is this!" He held it out and stabbed his thumb on the front page. "This is all lies."

"No, it isn't." Jude found his voice. "I saw the plans when they fell out of your briefcase."

This time it was Guy Lipman's turn to stand there with his mouth open. He looked really guilty, and I knew that Jude hadn't made a mistake.

"What are you talking about?" he blustered.

People were starting to come out of their houses now to see what was going on. Mum hurried down our drive, followed more slowly by Grandpa and Grandma. Mr Hart flung open a bedroom window and peered out of Number Three, and Mrs Crumble was standing on her doorstep. The Cubbs, too, had come outside.

"We know what you're up to," Tiger said, "and you're not going to get away with it!"

"We don't want a supermarket here," Mrs Cubb added.

"We'll fight you every step of the way," said Tiger's dad.

"Oh really?" snapped Mr Lipman. "Well, let me tell you something. Mrs Dawkins phoned me last night and asked me to bring the contract over nice and early." He turned and pulled his briefcase out of the car. "She wants to get the signing over and done with." He gave us a silky smile. "So if you'll just get out of my way, I'll get on with it." He pushed past us, giving us a smug glance. "As if anyone is going to take any notice of your silly little newspaper anyway..."

Tiger made to run after him up the garden path, but her mum stopped her. "We've got to speak to Mrs Dawkins," Tiger cried.

"Tiger, she can sell the fields to whomever she likes," Mrs Cubb said gently.

"But that doesn't mean we have to sit back and let *him* do whatever he likes," Tiger's dad added. "We can form a protest group. Stop him getting planning permission."

"But Mr Lipman's got the plans," Jude said anxiously. "He must be pretty sure that he can get permission if he *does* buy the fields."

Suddenly a loud noise made us all turn round. It was the sound of marching feet. We watched in amazement as a large crowd of people turned the corner from Love Lane into Cosy Crescent and marched towards us. The crescent was quickly full to overflowing with all sorts of people – old, young, men, women and kids. Some of them carried banners reading *Save our Fields.* And a lot of them were carrying copies of a newspaper — *our* newspaper!

A man at the front of the crowd stepped forward. "Are we too late to stop the land from being sold?" he asked. I recognised him as the man I'd spoken to on the fields yesterday.

"That's why *he's* here," Jude replied, pointing at Mr Lipman, who was standing by Mrs D.'s door looking completely shocked.

"No supermarket on our fields!" someone shouted, and everyone cheered. I grinned at Jude, Tiger and the others. So our newspaper *had* done some good.

"It looks like you've really started something here," remarked Mum, coming over to join us. "Good job I didn't recycle those papers!"

I didn't think the crescent could get any more crowded, but then the cars started appearing. At the front I recognised Lynn's bright-pink old banger. I could see Billy the greyhound curled up on the back seat. But she wasn't the only one. There were five or six other cars behind her. The crowd parted and shuffled to one side so that the cars could draw up at the kerb.

"Hello, Mr Lipman," Lynn called, as she climbed out of her car. "Remember me? I was one of those people who protested about you closing the animal sanctuary in Trimbledale. And my friends and I have brought along some of the animals you made homeless."

She turned to let Billy out. The other people began to get out of their cars too. They all had dogs, and one woman even had two cats in a basket! I couldn't help staring at Guy Lipman. He looked as if he just couldn't believe his eyes.

"I—I did no such thing," he stammered weakly.

Suddenly the front door of Number Five flew open, and Mrs Dawkins appeared on the doorstep.

"What's going on here?" she demanded.

Chapter Ten

The whole crowd fell silent as Mrs Dawkins glared round at everyone. She was dressed in her usual layers of shawls and cardigans, but today she was wearing a floppy black hat with a red ribbon tied round it.

"I said, what's going on here?" she repeated. Then she caught sight of one of the banners. "*Save our fields*," she read out. Then she scowled. "The fields are mine," she said abruptly. "And it's up to me what I do with them."

Mr Lipman had recovered a bit by now and was smiling smugly again. "Why don't we go inside and get down to business," he began.

"No!" said Sugar and Spice loudly, forgetting for once that they were scared of Mrs Dawkins!

"We just want you to know what Mr Lipman's *really* going to use the fields for," Tiger said earnestly.

"Did you read the newspaper?" I asked.

Mrs Dawkins didn't reply.

"It's all nonsense!" blustered Guy Lipman, slowly turning purple in the face. "I've never heard anything so—"

"Lynn can tell you all about what Guy Lipman's really like," Jude cut in.

"Just listen to her," Flash pleaded.

"Please, Mrs Dawkins," Cookie said softly.

For a moment I thought Mrs Dawkins was going to go back inside, taking Mr Lipman with her, and shut the door on us. But then she folded her arms and stared at Lynn who had stepped forward. As Lynn explained about the animal sanctuary, the expression on Mrs Dawkins' face didn't change one bit. I wasn't sure whether she believed us or not, or even if she was listening.

"Maybe you don't want to believe this," Lynn ended up, "but I can tell you that Guy Lipman is not to be trusted."

There was silence when Lynn had finished speaking. No one made a sound. I held my breath, wondering what Mrs Dawkins would decide.

She turned to Guy Lipman.

"Give me the contract," she said gruffly.

Smirking, Mr Lipman clicked open his briefcase and

pulled out a bulky document.

"I'm glad you've seen sense, Mrs Dawkins," he said smugly. "And I can assure you that there is no truth in anything these people have been saying."

Then his eyes almost popped out of his head as Mrs Dawkins turned away, ripped the contract in half, lifted the lid of her wheelie bin and dropped the torn pages inside!

A huge cheer went up. Jude slapped me on the back, grinning all over his face. Cookie threw her arms round Flash who swung her off her feet, and the twins linked hands and danced up and down. Tiger hurried past Guy Lipman who was stalking furiously back to his car, ran up to Mrs Dawkins and flung her arms round her.

"Thank you!" she said gratefully

Mrs Dawkins looked a bit embarrassed but very pleased. "If I ever decide to sell the fields," she said, "I'll talk to people in Sunnyvale first."

Guy Lipman climbed into his car and banged the door shut behind him. There was another cheer as he put his foot down and drove angrily out of the crescent.

"Well, let's hope that's the last we'll see of *him!*" said Mrs Cubb.

The crowd of people was beginning to drift away now, all looking very pleased with the way things had turned out. Tiger's parents invited Lynn and her friends (and their animals) into the Cubbs' house for a cup of tea, and our mum and grandparents went too. Mrs Dawkins scooped up a couple of her cats who had escaped into the front garden and went back inside. Soon there was only us left.

"I reckon we deserve a bit of a celebration," Jude announced.

We all trooped back to the garage, and Jude and I raided the kitchen for chocolate and bottles of lemonade. Mum was over at the Cubbs' place, but we didn't think she'd mind.

"Here's to our newspaper!" Tiger laughed, raising her glass of lemonade in a toast.

"And let's hope there's lots more of them!" I added.

Jude groaned. "We've only just finished the *first* issue," he pointed out. "We need a bit of a break."

"We've got to get some more ideas," Sugar said.

"Yeah, I'm all puzzled out!" Spice grinned.

"And we're never going to top the first one anyway," Flash chimed in. "It was mega when all those people turned up."

Cookie nodded. "We'll have to work really hard to make the next issue just as good."

"And that's why we need to start working on it right now," I told everyone with a grin. "So start thinking!"

⊙ bang on the door ™ ©

friends

Together we make things happen!

Follow the further adventures of Spex, Jude, Tiger, Sugar, Spice, Flash and Cookie, as they report on more exciting goings on in their ace newspaper the *Sunnyvale Standard*

FRIENDS UNITED

Disaster! The local pool has been closed down – and just before the summer hols! It's a race against time as the Friends swing into action to save their pool.

And coming soon...

FRIENDS AGAIN

The Friends discover local animals are in danger and tempers are running high. Can they pull together... and catch the culprit?

An imprint of HarperCollins*Publishers*

bang on the door™©

silly billy

Follow the adventures of Silly Billy –
the silliest boy in the WHOLE world.

TIME OUT

Silly Billy has a brand new watch...
But he doesn't quite know how to use it.
When its alarm goes off one hour early
Silly Billy decides to get HIMSELF
ready for school. And that's when the
trouble starts...

And coming soon...

POOL FOOL

An imprint of HarperCollins*Publishers*

ⓐ bang on the door™ ©

poo jokebook
Every pun is guaranteed to pong
in this stinky collection!

What do you get if you cross an
elephant with a bottle of laxative?
Out of the way!

What do you get if you eat baked
beans and onions?
Tear gas!

Packed with wicked whiffs, real stinkers and
nasty niffs – jokes that will run and run!

Collins

An imprint of HarperCollins*Publishers*

⊚ bang on the door ™ ©

Collect 5 tokens and get a free poster!*

All you have to do is collect five funky tokens!
You can snip one from any of these cool Bang on the Door books!

0 00 715209 4

0 00 715309 0

0 00 715212 4

0 00 715210 8

Send 5 tokens with a completed coupon to: Bang on the Door Poster Offer

PO Box 142, Horsham, RH13 5FJ (UK residents)

c/- HarperCollins Publishers (NZ) Ltd,
PO Box 1, Auckland (NZ residents)

c/- HarperCollins Publishers, PO Box 321,
Pymble NSW 2073, Australia
(for Australian residents)

0 00 715220 5

First name: .... Surname: ....

Address: ....

....

....

Postcode: .... Child's date of birth: .... / .... / ....

email address: ....

Signature of parent/guardian: ....

Tick here if you do not wish to receive further information about children's books ☐

F1

1 token